ALLIGATOR SHOES

by Arthur Dorros

PUFFIN BOOKS

for Brian,
Ellen, Carol, Dave C.,
and Dave D.

Copyright © 1982 by Arthur Dorros
All rights reserved.
Unicorn is a registered trademark of Dutton Children's Books.
Library of Congress number 82-2409
ISBN 978-0-14-054734-4
Published in the United States by
Dutton Children's Books,
a member of Penguin Putnam Inc.
345 Hudson Street, New York, New York 10014
Editor: Ann Durell   Designer: Claire Counihan
Manufactured in China by South China Printing Co.
First Unicorn Edition 1988
27 28 29 30

Alvin was an alligator.

He liked watching people.
Mostly he saw feet.

"Maybe I'll get some shoes,"
thought Alvin. "But what kind?"

He went to the shoe store.
He looked at shoes and shoes.
The store closed.

"I'm locked in!" said Alvin.

"I'll try on shoes," he decided.

He tried on cowboy boots,

running shoes,

dancing shoes,

hiking shoes,

climbing shoes,

basketball shoes,

rain shoes,

plain shoes,

going-on-the-train shoes,

and sandals.

Then he fell asleep.

In the morning, when he woke up,
someone was holding his foot.

"I like these alligator shoes,"
  she said.

"These are not alligator shoes.
They are alligator feet!"
said Alvin.

And he walked home.

"I like alligator feet,"
said Alvin, "better than
alligator shoes."